THIS CANDLEWICK BOOK BELONGS TO:

First U.S. paperback edition 1996

ISBN 1-56402-591-8

2 4 6 8 10 9 7 5 3 1

Printed in Hong Kong

The pictures in this book were done in watercolor and ink.

Candlewick Press
2067 Massachusetts Avenue
Cambridge, Massachusetts 02140

A Busy Day
at the
Airport

PHILIPPE DUPASQUIER

CANDLEWICK PRESS
CAMBRIDGE, MASSACHUSETTS

Who gets to the airport first in the morning?

Why, Sylvester Dustpan, of course.

Mr. Countalot, a very rich and busy man,
runs to board his private plane.

Sylvester sweeps up the viewing area.

Sidney tows the jet from its hangar.

Sam gets the stairway.

Captain Cloudy and his crew arrive.

"Can I have some money for the telescope?"
Tom asks his dad.

Many people are leaving and many stay behind.
Some load the bags and some fuel the jet.

Jim and Arthur, noisy brothers, pretend
to be noisy planes.

CHP! CHP! CHP! CHP! CHP! goes the helicopter!

EE-AA! EE-AA! EE-AA! goes the ambulance!

RRRRRRRRRROOAARRR goes the jet, taking off.

Tom shouts something, but no one hears.

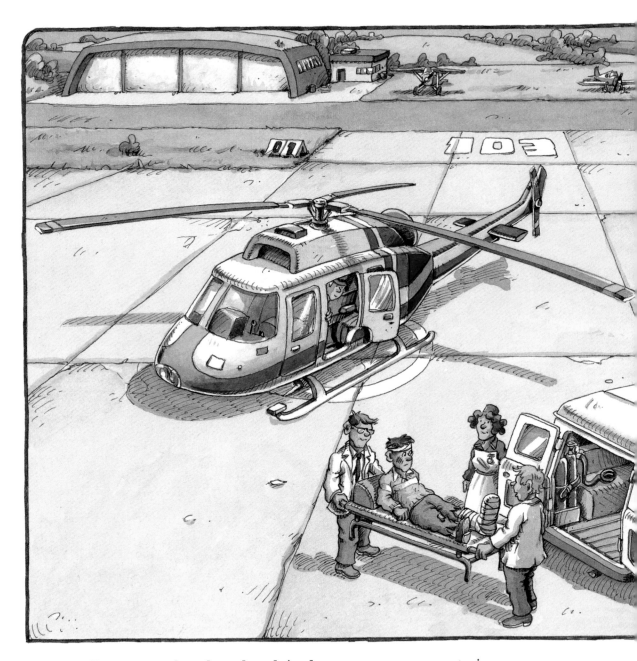

Peter Percy, who broke his leg on a mountain,
is carried to the ambulance.

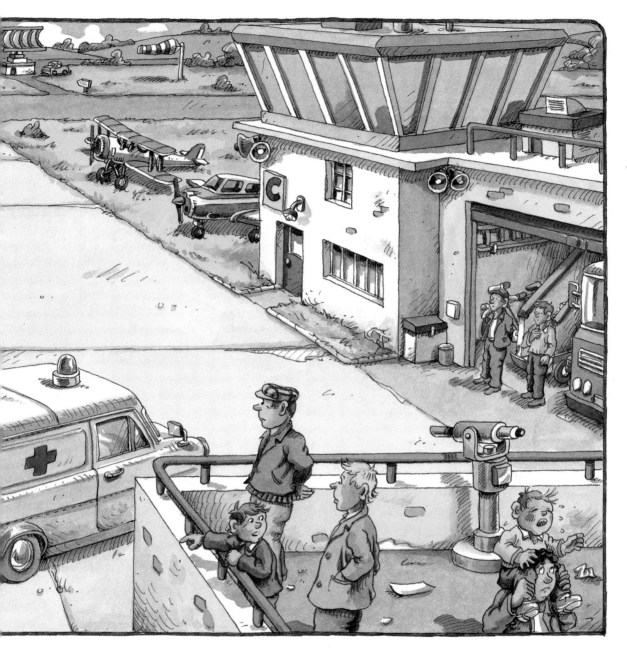

Timothy Toddle, who didn't like all the noise,
is carried home.

Line up the band! Roll out the red carpet!

Get the security guards in position!

Clear the viewing area! Someone extremely
important is landing now.

The band strikes up, all except for the tuba
player, who is late. The doors of the plane
open. The cameras begin to click.

"Welcome, Mr. Lemon Dropp, Greatest Candy Maker
in the World! And your lovely wife Lollipop!
And your brother Arnie! And his best friend Wally!"

Mr. Countalot comes home, a little richer than before. "What a busy day!" he says.

Sylvester sweeps up the viewing area again.

The ground crew locks up and heads for home.

Who plays with paper planes when the day
is done? Who leaves the airport last?

Why, Sylvester Dustpan, of course.

IF THIS BOOK IS ONE OF YOUR CHILD'S FAVORITES, WHY NOT BUY
ANOTHER COPY TO PUT SAFELY ASIDE AS A KEEPSAKE?
YOUR CHILD AND YOUR CHILD'S CHILDREN WILL THANK YOU!

PHILIPPE DUPASQUIER studied illustration and advertising in France.
While in college, he spent three months in England, and was so impressed
by the quality of illustration there that he decided to move there. He says
his style was influenced in part by his long fascination with comics.
"[They] have always been important to me, and in France they are are a
recognized form of illustration." Philippe Dupasquier is the author of
many books for children, including the award-winning *Dear Daddy*.